The Rise of Voltron

Adapted by Cala Spinner

Simon Spotlight

New York London Toronto Sydney New Delhi

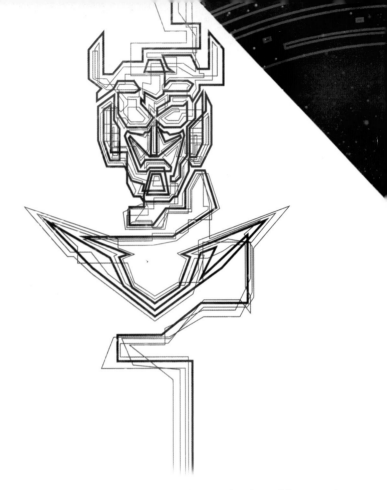

SIMON SPOTLIGHT
An imprint of Simon & Schuster Children's Publishing Division
1230 Avenue of the Americas, New York, New York 10020
This Simon Spotlight edition August 2017
DreamWorks Voltron Legendary Defender © 2017 DreamWorks Animation LLC. TM World Events Productions, LLC. All Rights Reserved. All rights reserved, including the right of reproduction in whole or in part in any form. SIMON SPOTLIGHT and colophon are registered trademarks of Simon & Schuster, Inc. For information about special discounts for bulk purchases, please contact Simon & Schuster Special Sales at 1-866-506-1949 or business@simonandschuster.com.
Designed by Nick Sciacca and Brittany Naundorff. The text of this book was set in United Sans Reg.
Manufactured in the United States of America 0617 LAK
2 4 6 8 10 9 7 5 3 1
ISBN 978-1-5344-0920-0 (hc)
ISBN 978-1-5344-0919-4 (pbk)
ISBN 978-1-5344-0921-7 (eBook)

CHAPTER 1

"Flight log 5-11-14. Begin descent to Kerberos for rescue mission," said Lance.

Lance was a student at a school for space travel called the Galaxy Garrison. He was studying to be a pilot—and taking an important simulation test.

"Lance, can you keep this thing straight?" said Hunk, one of Lance's classmates.

Poor Hunk looked like he was about to throw up.

"Relax, Hunk. It's not like I did this," Lance said. He sped up the mock-spaceship. "Or *this*!" He made a sharp dive.

"Unless you want to wipe beef Stroganoff out of this thing, you better knock it off," Hunk said.

Hunk *really* didn't want to throw up.

"We've picked up a distress signal," said Pidge, another of Lance's classmates.

The distress signal was part of the test. The test was a rescue simulation for the missing crew of the Kerberos Mission. If Lance, Hunk, and Pidge completed the rescue simulation, they'd pass the test.

Unfortunately, the mock-spaceship started shaking.

"Oh no," Hunk grumbled.

Blech! He barfed right into the main gearbox.

The shaking got worse, and Lance lost control of the ship.

Smash! The ship crashed into the surface of the moon.

"Simulation failed," the computer beeped.

The test was over.

After the day's failure, Lance decided it was time for some team bonding. Lance and Hunk snuck out of their bunks to hang with Pidge. Except Pidge wasn't in the bunks like the rest of the students—Pidge was on the rooftop of the Garrison, surrounded by lots of fancy tech.

"Where'd you get this stuff?" Lance asked.

"I built it," Pidge admitted. "With this thing, I can scan all the way to the edge of the solar system."

"All the way to Kerberos?"

Pidge looked surprised.

Lance had noticed that Pidge acted strange every time someone brought up the Kerberos Mission.

"What's your deal?" he asked. "Look, Pidge, if we're going to bond as a team, we can't have any secrets."

Pidge thought for a moment.

"Fine. The world as you know it is about to change," Pidge said. "The Kerberos Mission wasn't lost because of some malfunction or crew mistake. I've been scanning the

system and picking up alien radio chatter."

"Aliens?" Hunk asked.

Pidge nodded. "They keep repeating one word: 'Voltron.'"

Beep! Beep! Beep!

As if on cue, an alarm blared overhead.

"What's going on?" Hunk asked. "Is that a meteor?"

An object soared in the sky. It got closer by the second.

"It's a ship," Pidge announced.

It was an *alien* ship. It crashed not too far away.

Hunk, Pidge, and Lance fled the rooftop. They had to see more.

The pilot aboard the alien ship was brought inside the Garrison's hospital. Guards stood outside, but Pidge accessed an internal camera so they could take a closer look.

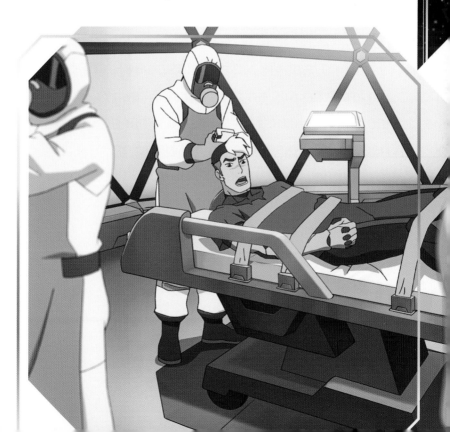

Lance recognized the person as Shiro, the pilot of the missing Kerberos Mission. Shiro looked weak, and mysteriously, his right arm had been replaced with a robotic one.

"Aliens are coming!" Shiro yelled. "We have to find Voltron."

"Voltron," Pidge repeated.

It was the same word that Pidge had picked up earlier.

But the doctors wanted to run tests on Shiro—not listen to him.

"We have to get him out," said Pidge.

The only question was, how?

Boom! Boom! Boom!

While they considered how to rescue Shiro, explosions erupted outside. All of the guards ran toward the blasts.

"Are those the aliens? Are they here? They got here so quick!" Hunk yelled.

Pidge looked out in the distance.

"No, those explosions were a distraction—for him."

Someone piloted in from the other direction.

"No way! That guy is always trying to one-up me," Lance said.

"Who is it?" asked Hunk.

"Keith," said Lance. "I'd recognize that mullet anywhere."

Keith was a former student at the Garrison. He was the best pilot at school, but flunked out because of a discipline issue. Keith rushed into the room where Shiro was being held and freed him from the straps holding him to the hospital cot. Then he slung Shiro over his shoulder.

Just then, Lance, Hunk, and Pidge burst in.

"Nope. No you don't. *I'm* saving Shiro," Lance said. He grabbed Shiro's other arm.

"Who are you?" Keith asked.

"Who am I? Uh, the name is Lance. We were in the same class at the Garrison."

Keith barely remembered Lance, but he didn't have time to argue.

They carried Shiro away and brought him to Keith's outpost for recovery.

CHAPTER 2

By sunrise, Shiro was feeling better.

But Shiro's head was still scrambled. He didn't know where he'd been for the past year. All he knew was that aliens had captured him and he'd somehow escaped.

"Did anyone else from your crew make it out?" Pidge asked.

Unfortunately, Shiro only remembered bits and pieces. "I remember the word 'Voltron.' It's some kind of weapon the aliens are looking for, but I don't know why. Whatever it is, I think we need to find it before they do."

"Well, last night I was rummaging through Pidge's stuff—" Hunk began.

Pidge cut him off. "What were you doing in my stuff?"

"I was looking for a candy bar, but then I started reading his diary, and I noticed that the repeating series of numbers the aliens are searching for looks like a Fraunhofer line," Hunk said.

A Fraunhofer line, Hunk explained, showed how much energy something has.

"Hunk, you big gassy genius!" Lance said.

Hunk took out a drawing he made of the Fraunhofer line. Keith held it up to a map of a cave he'd been researching. The points lined up.

It was too much of a coincidence—the team had to visit the cave. But what would they find?

The cave was covered in mysterious carvings of lions. When Keith touched them, nothing happened. But when Lance did, they lit up.

Crash!

Suddenly, the ground beneath them opened, and everyone fell through.

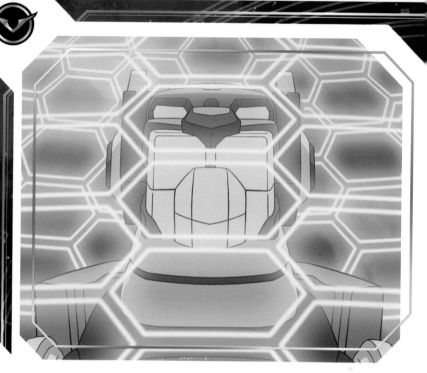

At the bottom of the cave was a giant robotic blue lion protected by a force field. It towered above them.

"Is this it? Is this the Voltron?" Pidge asked.

Keith put his hand on the force field. Nothing happened.

"Maybe you just have to knock," Lance said.

Lance pounded his fist against the force field.

To everyone's surprise, the lion's eyes flashed to life. The force field lowered. Then they each got a vision of five lions flying through space, forming one fearsome mega-robot. No doubt about it—the mega-robot was Voltron.

"Voltron is a huge, awesome robot," said Hunk.

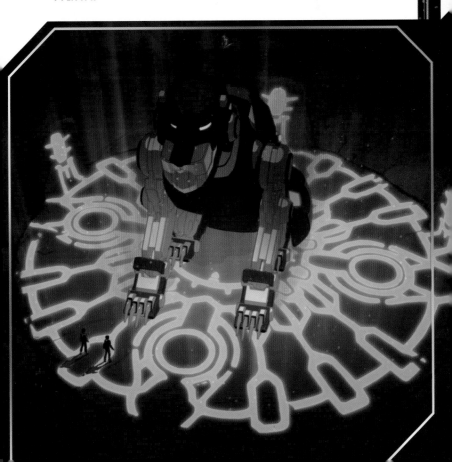

The lion opened its mouth, inviting every-one inside.

Lance wasn't afraid—he felt connected to the lion somehow. He walked in and took the pilot's seat.

The others followed.

"I think it's talking to me," Lance said.

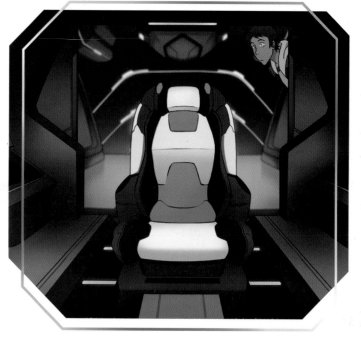

He grabbed the controls, and the lion rose up. Then it leaped out of the cave and started to fly!

"It says there's an alien ship approaching Earth," Lance explained. "I think we're supposed to stop it. The lion isn't saying words. . . . It's more like feeding ideas into my brain."

The lion flew into space. As it did, a giant alien spaceship approached and began to fire lasers at them.

Lance pulled another lever. The Blue Lion dodged the incoming beams.

"Let's try this," he said.

The lion returned laser fire. The alien ship was critically hit!

Now it was time to lure the aliens away from Earth. Lance piloted the lion away as the ship chased them.

The lion flew fast—faster than any other ship they'd been on. Suddenly, Shiro recognized the edge of the solar system.

"There's Kerberos," he said.

"It takes months for our ships to get out this far. We got out here in five seconds," observed Pidge.

The alien ship was gaining when a wormhole appeared before them.

"I think the lion wants us to go through there," Lance said.

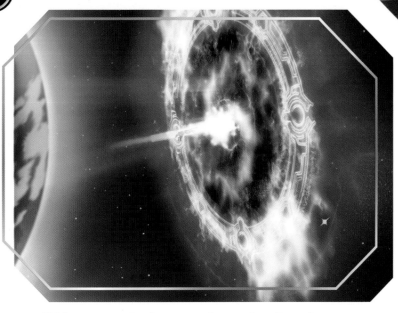

"Whatever is happening, the lion knows more than we do," said Shiro. "I say we trust it, but we're a team now. We should decide together."

Everyone nodded. They didn't know where the wormhole would take them, but they had no other choice.

"Guess we're all ditching class tomorrow," Lance said.

He piloted the lion into the center of the wormhole. It closed, and the alien spaceship was left behind.

CHAPTER 3

Blech! As soon as the team reached the other side of the wormhole, Hunk threw up.

"I'm surprised it took that long," Pidge said, looking the other way.

"We must be a long way from Earth," Shiro reasoned. He didn't recognize any of the stars they were passing.

The lion glided through space toward a tranquil-looking planet.

"The lion seems to want to go to this

planet. I think it's going home," Lance said.

They landed on a planet named Arus. The lion stopped in front of a giant Castle, and everyone walked in.

The Castle was empty aside from its control room, which housed two pods with bodies sleeping inside them.

"Are these guys dead?" Hunk asked.

It was a good question. No one had seen anything like this before.

Just then, one of the pods opened, revealing a tall teenage girl with long silvery hair. She was awake!

"Who are you?" the girl asked. "What are you doing in my castle?"

"A giant blue lion brought us here. That's all we know," said Lance.

The girl glared. "How do you have the Blue Lion? What happened to its Paladin?"

"We don't know what you're talking about," said Shiro. "Why don't you tell us who you are? Maybe we can help."

She introduced herself as Princess Allura of planet Altea. She had traveled far away from her home in the Castle, which was also a ship.

"I've got to find out where we are and how long we've been asleep," she said.

Allura activated a control board, displaying information. Immediately, the other pod opened, revealing a man named Coran.

"It can't be," Allura said to Coran. "We've been asleep for ten thousand years!"

Allura's father, King Alfor, was gone. So was her planet—and everything else in her solar system. She and Coran—and the mice that had been with Allura in her pod—were the last Alteans alive.

Allura knew who was to blame.

"Zarkon," she said.

She explained that Zarkon was king of the Galra, an alien people bent on destroying worlds.

That made Shiro remember—he'd been Zarkon's prisoner!

Beep! Beep! Beep!

An alarm sounded.

"A Galra battleship has set its tracker to us," Coran announced.

"Good. Let them come. By the time they get here, you five will have reformed Voltron, and together we'll destroy Zarkon's empire," Allura said.

Allura explained that the only way to defeat Zarkon was to form Voltron—a super-weapon made up of five lions, including the Blue Lion. She believed the five of them were meant to pilot the lions as the Paladins of Voltron.

Each lion's personality, Allura explained, matched that of its Paladin.

"The Black Lion is the head of Voltron. It will take a pilot who is a born leader and in control at all times. Shiro, you will pilot the Black Lion," Allura said.

Shiro bowed.

"The Green Lion has a curious personality and needs a pilot of intellect and daring. Pidge, you will pilot the Green Lion."

Pidge smiled.

"The Blue Lion—"

"Let me guess. Takes the most handsome and best pilot of the bunch?" Lance asked.

Allura paused.

"The *Yellow* Lion," she continued, ignoring Lance, "is caring and kind. Its pilot is one who puts the needs of others above his own. As a leg of Voltron, you will lift the team up and hold them together."

Hunk knew it meant him.

"The Red Lion is temperamental and the most difficult to master. It's faster than the others, but also more unstable. Its pilot needs to be someone who relies more on instincts than skill. Keith, you will fly the Red Lion."

Keith nodded.

"Once all the lions are united, you will form Voltron, the most powerful warrior ever known—the Defender of the Universe."

Allura's father had scattered the lions to make sure Zarkon could never form Voltron. But now they needed to find them all.

Allura knew the locations of the Green, Yellow, and Black Lions. She showed every-one a map of where they were.

The Black Lion was locked in the Castle. But in order to be freed, the other four lions needed to be present.

Unfortunately, Allura could not locate the Red Lion's coordinates yet. She promised to keep trying.

There was no time to waste. The team split up to collect the lions—they knew what had to be done.

CHAPTER 4

After Pidge and Hunk collected their lions, everyone returned to Arus. The only lion left to find before they could free the Black Lion was the Red Lion. Princess Allura had discovered its location. It was stuck on a Galran spaceship—the very spaceship that was approaching.

As the Paladins discussed how to retrieve the lion and destroy the ship, a message appeared overhead. It was from

Commander Sendak, one of Zarkon's men. Sendak was in charge of the nearby Galran ship.

"I am here to confiscate the lions," Sendak announced. "Turn them over to me, or I will destroy your planet."

Turning over the lions was admitting defeat. They couldn't do that. If the Galra had the lions and could form Voltron, they would be capable of destroying Arus, Earth, and any other planet in their wake.

Princess Allura decided to activate the Castle's force field. It wouldn't keep Sendak away forever, but it would hold him off until they figured out a plan.

Shiro turned to Princess Allura.

"What do you think is the best course of action?" he asked.

Princess Allura didn't know.

"Perhaps your father can help," Coran suggested. He explained that King Alfor stored his memories in a supercomputer in the Castle.

Coran brought Allura to the supercomputer. A hologram of King Alfor appeared before her.

Allura beamed with happiness. She missed her father very much.

"Forming Voltron is the only way to stop Zarkon," the hologram of King Alfor said. It was clear he regretted scattering the lions ten thousand years ago. "You must be willing to sacrifice everything to assemble the lions."

Allura reached out her hand. For a brief moment, she and her father held hands in the air. Then Allura stepped away from the hologram. She knew what the Paladins had to do.

"You were brought here for a reason," Allura said to the Paladins. "The Voltron lions are meant to be piloted by you. We must fight and keep fighting until we defeat Zarkon. It is our destiny."

Allura gave the Paladins their armor and their Bayards—the traditional weapons of the Voltron Paladins. Each Bayard took a different shape.

Hunk's Bayard was so big it almost made him topple over. Keith's Bayard was an unwieldy sword. Unfortunately, Shiro's Bayard was lost with its original Paladin. He would have to make do.

Allura briefed the Paladins on their mission—enter Sendak's ship and retrieve the Red Lion. She reminded Keith of the Red Lion's temperament.

"You'll have to earn its respect," she said.

Keith and the other Paladins were ready.

CHAPTER 5

While Hunk and Lance distracted Sendak by pretending to surrender, the other three Paladins entered the spaceship. Inside, Shiro realized something.

"I've been here before," he said. "The Galra brought me here."

Pidge wondered if Shiro's other crew-members from the Kerberos Mission were onboard.

"We've got to rescue them!" Pidge said.

But Shiro reminded Pidge that they didn't have time. "We have to get the Red Lion and return to Arus," he said.

"No!" yelled Pidge. "Commander Holt is my father. He and my brother were on the Kerberos Mission with you."

"Commander Holt is your father?" Shiro asked.

"Yes," said Pidge. "I'm not going to give up looking when I'm this close."

"I'm coming with you," Shiro said. "Keith, you go find the Red Lion."

Pidge wondered if Shiro knew the truth. Shiro had been with Pidge's father and brother on the Kerberos Mission. He might know that Commander Holt only had *one* son, Pidge's brother. Pidge was Commander Holt's *daughter*.

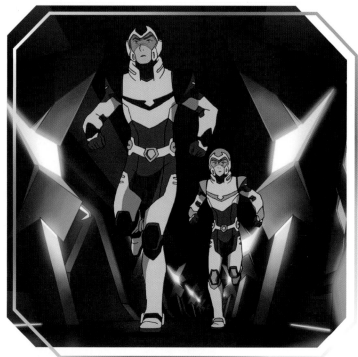

Pidge opened the prisoners' chamber. But her family wasn't there. Instead, there was a group of aliens. Some of them recognized Shiro. They called him "the Champion." Shiro didn't know why they called him that, but he didn't have time to figure it out. The Galran guards had found them!

Shiro used his robotic arm to ward off the Galran guards. He smashed, punched, and defeated the guards.

The former prisoners entered an escape pod and blasted away from the Galran ship. They were safe.

"Where did you learn to fight with that?" Pidge asked Shiro, nudging his robotic arm.

"No idea," he admitted.

It was like his arm had a mind of its own.

Meanwhile, Keith knew he didn't have much time. He was

about to give up when he closed his eyes and thought hard. Then he saw it in his mind—the Red Lion.

Keith's eyes popped open.

"Gotcha," he said, and started running toward its location.

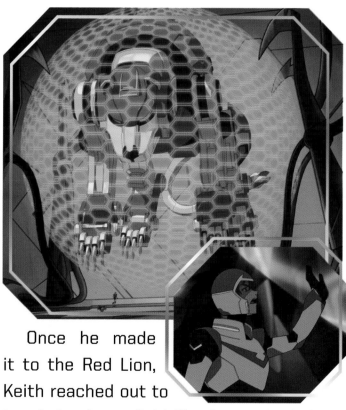

Once he made it to the Red Lion, Keith reached out to touch its force field like Lance had done with the Blue Lion, but nothing happened.

"It's me," he told the lion. "Keith. Your buddy."

The lion didn't budge.

"Come on. We're connected!" Keith pleaded with the lion.

The lion still wouldn't move.

Galran robots found him. Keith had no choice. He activated his Bayard and went after the robots.

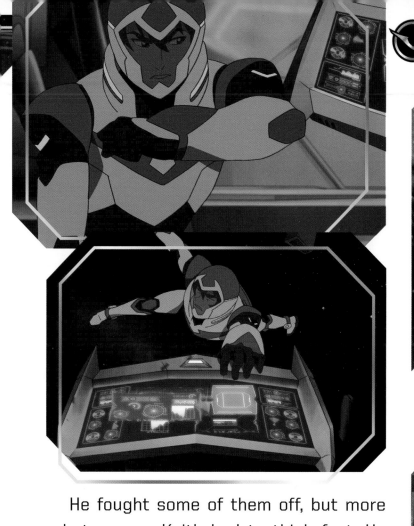

He fought some of them off, but more robots came. Keith had to think fast. He smashed a button, and the floor opened underneath them.

Crash! The robots fell into space.

Keith tried not to get sucked out too, but he lost his balance.

Just when all hope was lost, Keith saw something overhead.

It was the Red Lion!

The lion opened its mouth and grabbed Keith, saving him. The Red Lion met up with the other lions. They had all escaped the Galran ship.

Now there was only one thing left to do.

Shiro had to collect the Black Lion.

CHAPTER 6

The Paladins flew back to Arus. When they arrived, the Black Lion sensed the others. *Roar!* It came to life. Shiro marched into the lion through its open mouth. After 10,000 years, the Voltron lions were together again.

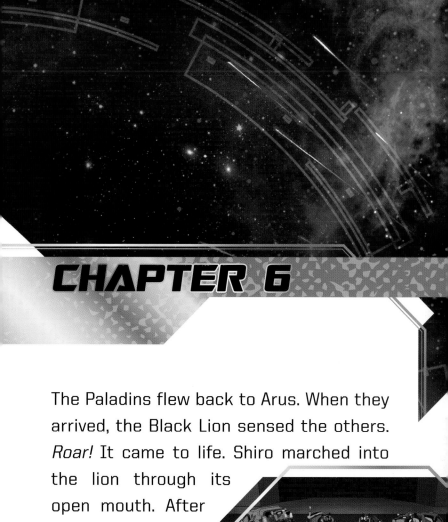

But all was not well. Sendak's ship

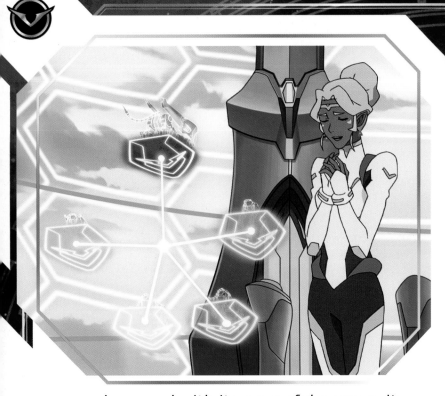

was close, and with its powerful cannon, it could destroy the Castle—and Arus—at any moment.

Allura let the Paladins know they needed to form Voltron—*now.*

"Listen up, team. The only way to succeed is to give it all you've got," Shiro said.

The other Paladins agreed. They were in this together. But they didn't know how to form Voltron.

"I don't see a 'combine into giant robot' button," Hunk said.

Shiro suggested that everyone fly in formation. "One, two, three, Voltron!"

The five lions leaped into the air while dodging laser fire from smaller Galran ships. The lions flew higher and higher—but nothing happened. Instead, they got sucked into the tractor beam of the huge Galran ship.

It seemed like all was lost. Sendak would claim the lions—and Voltron—for Emperor Zarkon and the Galra Empire.

But Shiro didn't give up hope.

"We can do this," Shiro said. "We have to believe in ourselves. We're the universe's only hope. If we work together, we'll win together."

The Paladins were reenergized by Shiro's speech.

"Yeah!" they said together.

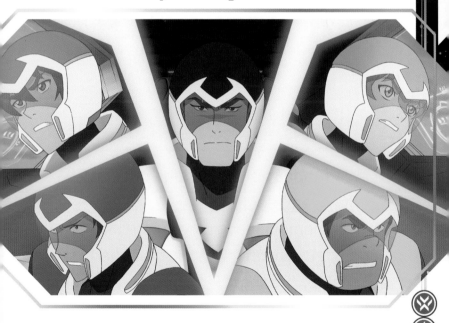

And that was the secret to forming Voltron: teamwork. The lions roared—and transformed into the super-robot!

"I can't believe it," Keith said.

"We formed Voltron!" Pidge shouted.

"I'm a leg!" said Hunk.

Shiro commanded everyone to take down Sendak's cannon. Voltron punched the spaceship, tearing the cannon to shreds. Lasers shot out of Voltron's arms, blasting holes

through the Galran ship. Sendak realized he had lost and escaped on one of the smaller ships. As he fled, Voltron tore through the big ship until there was nothing left.

There was no doubt about it. Voltron was *strong*.

"We did it," Shiro said.

Back on Arus, Allura and Coran cheered. They'd lived to fight another day.

But until Zarkon and his empire were defeated, there would be more battles to fight. *Many* more battles to fight. Allura knew that Zarkon wouldn't stop until he had the five lions. He would already be planning his next move . . . sending something even more terrifying than Sendak's giant ship with its cannon capable of destroying planets. This was just the beginning.

"It's not going to be easy being the Defenders of the Universe," said Coran.

"Defenders of the Universe, huh?" said Shiro. "That's got a nice ring to it."

Voltron had risen again.

Get ready for another legendary adventure in

Battle for the Black Lion!

"Thanks to Pidge's modifications, we'll have thirty seconds of cloaking," Shiro said as the Green Lion disappeared into the background of stars.

The five Paladins of Voltron and Princess Allura gathered their courage as they flew from the Castle of Lions to a secret transportation hub of the Galra Empire.

They landed on a craggy moon covered with machinery and snuck on to the base undetected.

When they reached the central control room, the Paladins drew their Bayards. Hunk and Lance's Bayards transformed into energy blasters. Hunk kicked down the door, and with two easy shots, he and Lance took out the robotic henchmen. The rest of the team streamed into the room.

Shiro, the Black Paladin, didn't have a Bayard. He knocked out the Galra lieutenant with his energy hand. Princess Allura restrained the lieutenant with energy cuffs.

Keith covered the door with his Red Bayard, which had transformed into a sword.

The room was clear. Pidge's *katar* transformed back into her Green Bayard. She quickly unpacked the tech she'd made for the mission.

"We only have a few minutes before the next patrol comes by," Shiro told the team. He had been a Galra prisoner and remembered the sentries' patrol pattern. "But that should be enough to get what we need," he continued.

Pidge connected her device to the control room computer, then to Shiro's robotic arm. The Galra had transformed his arm while he was their prisoner. It was a constant reminder of the Galra's cruelty, but it also allowed the team to interface with Galra tech. "I've made some software modifications since the last time we tried to download Galra info," Pidge said.

Now was the moment of truth. The team took a big risk sneaking on to a Galra base. They needed information if they were ever going to stop Emperor Zarkon from conquering the universe. . . .